I0841064

"The first thing to note about this book is its ability to draw young readers into the intriguing world of five friends whose efforts to play hide-and-seek result in an experience that tests their confidence in reality itself: 'Have you ever been somewhere you thought you knew, down to the tiniest detail, only to discover that things are not at all as they seem?' The first-person game turns into a journey none of the kids expected in a story punctuated by color drawings that bring the chapters to life."

- D. Donovan, Senior Reviewer, Midwest Book Review

"What sets this book apart is its attention to detail and historical accuracy. The author has clearly done extensive research to ensure that each period is accurately portrayed, which makes the story all the more immersive. The characters are well-developed and relatable, and their adventures are exciting and unpredictable. From the forests of pre-Columbian America to the battlefields of World War II, this book takes the reader on a journey through time that is both thrilling and enlightening."

- Booklife by Publishers Weekly

"Find Me in Time: Meeting Columbus is a thrilling adventure that takes readers on a journey through time and history. It's a story that challenges readers to think critically about the past and to question the narratives they've been taught. With its engaging characters and exciting plot, this book is sure to capture the imagination of young readers and spark their curiosity about the world around them."

- Readers' Choice Book Awards

"Find Me In Time: Meeting Columbus is a fantastic adventure that not only takes readers on a thrilling time-travel journey but also provides an educational look at the history of Christopher Columbus and the impact of his actions on the native peoples he encountered. The vivid descriptions of the past and the interactions between the characters and historical figures make this a captivating read for children and adults alike. I highly recommend this book to anyone looking for a fun and informative way to learn about history."

- Kameron Brook, Reviewer, Reedsy Discovery

"Find Me In Time is a wildly entertaining story that will keep kids paying attention to every page as they tour history in a brand-new way. L.T. Caton is either a history buff or has spent some serious time researching the places, times, and history that happen in each location. I highly recommend it to those who are adventurous or who enjoy history."

- Amy Raines, Readers' Favorite

"From the first scene, L.T. Caton wraps us in the plot and characters. The detailed illustrations help us see the story as it unfolds and give it depth. The culture and language of the Taino people are seamlessly woven into the story, giving us a better picture of the natives and what shaped their lives. Children may have a different view of Christopher Columbus, but after understanding the heartbreaking actual events around his exploration, they may form an alternate opinion. Find Me In Time: Meeting Columbus is a beautiful story for older children, which offers a different perspective of Columbus's exploration."

- Courtnee Turner Hoyle, Readers' Favorite

"L.T. Caton loves history; her desire is to allow her love of the subject to become infectious. In Find Me In Time, she meets her goal to make history come alive and exciting. Using time travel, through the larger inside than outside TreeHouse, five children learn that history has some dark edges. While entertaining, it also teaches lessons from history. For instance, your child will learn that the word 'hammock' originally came from the Taino people, the first Americans Columbus met. Who wouldn't want to travel back in history and witness events as they happened? This story gives you that opportunity. I recommend it to help children become interested in history."

- Philip Van Heusen, Readers' Favorite

"Caton's engaging work of historical fiction, aimed primarily at children and young readers, offers a concise and enlightening history lesson accessible to all. This compelling book provides an informative and eye-opening account of natural history, presented in a manner that is neither tedious nor traumatizing. The story is skillfully crafted, with a well-paced plot that smoothly transitions from one event to another. While the characters may not be intricate, their warm, genuine friendship dynamic underscores children's inclusivity and open-mindedness when unencumbered by adult biases."

- Karen Almeida, Assistant Editor, Literary Titan

"A fast-moving and culturally aware adventure that offers a well-pitched introduction to historical investigation."

- Kirkus Review

"Find Me In Time: Meeting Columbus" by L.T. Caton engages the reader with pages full of action-packed scenes, educates students and adults with well-researched historical facts, and captivates the reader with the emotions her story brings to life. Ms. Caton expertly times her action scenes, bringing the characters back to safety yet leaving the reader on a cliffhanger, hungering for more. I was impressed that a book geared toward middle school-age children made me question what I learned throughout my education. I look forward to reading more from this author and plan to incorporate her 'Find Me In Time' series into our home library."

- Leigh Kimberly Zoby, Reader Views

FIND ME IN TIME

Meeting Columbus

L. T. Caton

Illustrated by Naheed Hayder

To my parents, Bernard and Marcia Caton, I would not have had the opportunity to achieve my dreams without your hard work, sacrifice, support, and unwavering love.

MEET THE CHARACTERS

Harry

Harry used to be bullied for being overweight, but he has a good sense of humor and can almost always manage a smile. He loves inviting friends to his house where they can hang out in the pool or game room. Harry has freckles, ginger hair, and wears fashionable glasses.

Keith

Keith is confident and protective of his friends. He enjoys drawing and has a passion for architecture, dreaming of one-day designing buildings. His peers often seek his advice in resolving conflicts due to his level-headed nature. He always wears fashionable clothes that match his well-kept buzz-cut afro.

Ashley

Ashley has always been a bit shy, hiding in her hoodie and only speaking when she has something really important to say. She tends to notice things no one else does and really cares about people. Her family is from Puerto Rico and they speak Spanish at home. She's not very tall, but she's easy to spot with her bunches of curly hair.

Aaron

Aaron is smart and athletic, but he's sometimes impulsive when he should take time to think ahead. He likes to solve puzzles and has a competitive spirit. He's a fashion-free zone and always dresses in comfy jeans and tee shirts. He has a mop of dark hair that almost covers his forehead and bright green eyes.

Emma

Emma manages to stay organized even when the unexpected happens. Her friends can count on her to find the answers to just about any question. She lives in a small apartment with her younger sister and her mom. She loves finding new ways to wear thrift store clothes and can almost always be found in a well-pressed skirt that matches her tidy blonde hair.

Table of Contents

Prologue

Have you ever been somewhere you thought you knew, down to the tiniest detail, only to discover that things are not at all as they seem?

It started out as just another normal day for Ashley, Emma, Keith, Aaron, and Harry, who had come to the woods to play hide-and-seek.

But Ashley and her friends were about to discover something incredible that would change their lives forever.

Chapter 1: Discovery

I was sure Harry had been right in front of us as we ran into the clearing, but now he was nowhere to be seen. As usual, we were playing after school in our favorite part of the woods.

"This is weird!" said Keith. "He was right there!" He ran his hand through his buzz-cut Afro, and I noticed his fashionable shirt had come untucked as he spun.

"I know," Emma replied, "it's as if he's disappeared into thin air!" She tucked her clean, thrift-store skirt behind her knees as she bent to look under a bush, careful not to snag her tidy blonde hair.

"Unlikely!" snorted Aaron, wiping his palms on his old jeans, leaving smears of dust. "Harry's too, um, solid to suddenly become invisible!"

"Aaron, that's not kind!" said Emma, just as another voice exclaimed, "Hey!"

Harry's voice!

"Harry?!" we all shouted at once.

"Ye-es?" replied the voice, teasingly.

"Where are you? We can't see you!" I called.

There was no reply apart from a quiet snicker. I felt goose-flesh creep up my arms and the back of my neck, and I wished I had brought my hoodie to hug close. "Er, guys, this really is weird," I said. "How are we hearing him and not seeing him?"

Emma used her stern voice, "Harry, you're creeping Ashley out. Come out from wherever you're hiding."

"Oh, okay, you guys. Disculpa, Ash," came the voice again. I smiled at his choice to use Spanish to apologize. My friends were so considerate of my Puerto Rican heritage, but I still didn't have a clue where Harry could be. "Up here!" he said, and we looked up into the branches of the big old sycamore tree to see Harry's freckled face grinning down at us between the early summer leaves.

"But how —?" began Keith as we all stared, open-mouthed.

"You'll never guess what I found," said Harry, pushing his glasses back up his nose. "It's awesome! Look around the other side of the tree."

We trooped around the tree and saw a long ladder reaching up into the branches.

"But we know this place," said Aaron, shoving his messy mop of hair from his pale forehead, "and that's never been there before."

"And it looks old," Keith mused, "like it's been there a long time."

Keith was right. The ladder looked sturdy enough, but it was gnarled with age, and creepers had grown around some of the lower rungs.

"Come on up," said Harry. "You'll never believe what's up here!"

Keith went first, followed by Emma and me, then Aaron. When we reached a platform at the top of the ladder, we found Harry standing in front of a small treehouse.

"Welcome, my friends," he started in his best showman's voice, "to a wonder you will never forget!"

"How the—," "But—," "We'd have—," we all started saying at once.

"There's more," said Harry. "Come inside!"

"Huh?" said Aaron, flipping his hair out of his eyes. "I'm no scientist, but I can tell you that we won't all fit in there!"

"He's right, Harry," I said softly. "Maybe we can go one at a time."

"Okay," replied Harry, wiggling his eyebrows mysteriously, "but I think you'll be surprised." And with that, he disappeared into the treehouse.

Keith followed, and we heard him exclaim, "Wow! He's right—you really need to see this, guys!"

We looked at each other hesitantly, then followed Keith through the doorway.

I had to touch the wall nearest to me for balance as I tried to get my head around what I was seeing. The inside of the treehouse was huge! As big as our garage, at least! My neck prickled again, but I was more excited than spooked.

"This isn't," I started, "I mean, this is… like, magic, right?"

"It's gotta be," breathed Keith.

"I can't think of any rational explanation," said Emma.

"How did you find it, Harry?" asked Aaron, looking slightly dazed.

"Well, it was my turn to hide, remember?" started Harry. "And I ran into the clearing. I thought I'd hide in the bushes, but there were ants and bugs all over them, so I ran behind the tree. I closed my eyes, just for a second, and I thought, 'Please, please, don't let them find me,' and when I looked, the ladder was...just there in front of me. So I climbed up and found this place. Then you guys came, and you couldn't see me or the ladder." He giggled. "It was cool!"

We looked around the huge room. It was impossible that it could be this big, yet it was. It seemed to stretch way beyond the branches of the old sycamore tree. The floor and walls were made of long planks of wood. There were a few cobwebs in the corners, and it smelled like dust and stale air.

There were four windows, one on each side, all looking out onto thick leaves and branches. Pushing his head through one, Keith exclaimed, "There's a kind of platform all the way around the edge! How is that even possible?"

The rest of us clustered around him to look out. Then Emma went to the doorway and disappeared outside. Two seconds later, she stood on the other side of the window.

"It's, um, small again on the outside," she murmured, sounding far less certain than she usually did.

"Okay, this is cool!" Aaron declared. "This is seriously cool."

"What is this place?" I asked.

"I don't know," shrugged Keith, "but it doesn't look like anyone's been here in a long time."

"So now it's ours!" said Harry.

Emma came back in, and we all took a turn going outside onto the platform and walking around the treehouse. From the outside, it was the size of a small toolshed. Inside, it really was as big as a double garage. It made me feel dizzy stepping

in and out, so I went in and sat in the middle of the floor.

Soon the others joined me. We were all delighted with our discovery and started discussing how we could make it feel more like our place. I thought we could maybe haul some beanbags up, and Emma suggested bringing cooler boxes for food and drinks.

We were all making suggestions at once, laughing and joking, slightly breathlessly, when Harry blurted out, "You know what I'd really like to do? I'd like to find out when this place was built. I wish I knew who built it!"

As Harry spoke, the floor of the treehouse began to vibrate. We looked at each other, wide-eyed. I felt a falling motion in my stomach, and I let out a little scream.

"Oh no!" gasped Keith, "It's going to—"

But he didn't get to finish what he was saying because just then something happened that would change our lives forever.

Chapter 2:
A Hiding Place

The treehouse shook more and more violently. There was a deep rumbling sound as though the earth were growling, and bright lights flashed on and off in the windows. I thought we must be caught in an earthquake, and from what I could see of the others' faces in the flashing lights, I knew they were thinking the same thing. I grabbed on to Emma, who hugged me back fiercely. The boys crashed into each other as they tried to stay upright, but they all ended up crouching or lying on the floor. Just as I thought the treehouse was going to come crashing down, everything went dark. The shaking had stopped. I blinked, and suddenly I could see the treehouse again.

It was there, but it was different. For starters, it was dark except for a faint glow—moonlight?—coming in the door and windows. It smelled different too, like new wood, and the floor was rough and splintery under my knees. It wasn't as big as a garage anymore, either. It was about the size of a big garden shed, and the walls were closer to us as we sat, stunned by what had just happened.

We all looked at each other, then we all looked at Keith. He was the oldest, and he almost always knew what to do. At that moment, his brown eyes were as huge as plates.

"What the —" Harry started at the same time as Aaron said, "Whoa, was that an earthquake?"

"Sshhh!" hissed Keith urgently, nodding toward the door.

We all followed his gaze to see a dark shape looming in the doorway. For a moment, it blocked out the faint light, but as it moved into the treehouse, I could see that it was a man. He pulled something up into the treehouse, and I heard a rasping noise as the bulky object dragged against the edge of the doorway. A ladder. As my eyes began to get used to the dim light, I heard dogs barking and men shouting a little way off. Closer to us, there seemed to be a river or stream rushing.

The man began to speak. "The creek's burst its banks. That should help throw the dogs off our scent," he said in a deep, low voice. He was breathing heavily, and he was look- ing straight at us!

No. He was looking past us, somehow through us, at the far side of the treehouse. Slumped against the wall was a woman with a baby in her arms and two more children hud- dled against her. They all had dark skin, like Keith's, and the whites of the woman's terrified eyes glimmered in the gloom.

Harry let out a little yelp of fear, and Keith rose to his knees and spread his arms in front of us protectively. But neither the man nor the woman seemed to see or hear us. I could hear the sounds of voices and dogs coming closer. The wind was picking up outside, and rain started to beat against the roof. The woman moaned softly.

"Will the tree hold, even in the flood?" she whispered to the man.

"It should do. Try to stay calm. Keep them quiet," replied the man, nodding toward the children.

Aaron saw Keith's puzzled frown. "Hey, is that your dad?" he whispered.

Keith mumbled, "It's like...I don't know. I guess not. But it's...just like him."

The wind was howling now, and I heard a man shouting very close to the tree, "Trail's gone cold! Nowhere to hide here anyhow—too much water!"

A distant voice replied, and the barking started again in the distance. A dog barked right beneath the tree, making us all jump.

"Yeah, fine!" shouted the man below.

One of the children made a small whining sound. The mother held her closer to her body. Over the lashing of the rain and wind, I heard her whispered prayer, "Please, please, God, don't let them find us."

The treehouse started to shake. I looked at the others, alarmed that the storm would bring the tree down. Then the rumbling sound started again, just like it had before. The lights flashed faster and faster as the whole treehouse shook. Then everything went dark.

And then we were right back where we'd started. The tree-house was just like before: old, weathered wood, cobwebs and all. We looked at each other, but it was a minute before anyone spoke.

"Does anyone have any idea what just happened?" Aaron's face was even paler than usual, and his eyes were wide.

"Not really," I replied, "but it was really strange and really, really scary!"

"I think we went back in time!" Emma declared.

"Yeah, me too," Keith said. "What did you say just before it got weird, Harry?"

"Um, I think I said that I wanted to know when the treehouse was made and who'd made it," Harry said. "Then that happened."

"Those poor people," said Emma. "They were on the run, weren't they?"

"Yeah, from some bad people by the sound of it!" said Harry.

"I hope they got away," I said. "That man looked like you, Keith!" I added.

"Yeah...," Keith said, shaking his head. "Maybe one of my relatives. From the past."

"In the past, people used to build treehouses to keep families safe from wild animals and floods," mused Emma, "but this one must have been built to hide people."

"I'm just glad we left when we did!" Harry said. "It was getting pretty scary with those dogs and the storm."

"Maybe it's part of the magic?" Emma suggested. "Maybe it brings us back when it gets too scary. Strange!"

"So...do you think we could do it again?" asked Keith. "I

mean, could we go back in time to where we want, just by asking?"

"I guess there's only one way to find out," I answered.

I looked at Aaron, whose face was breaking into one of its rare smiles.

"You're right, Ash," he replied. "But where to go?"

I looked around as smiles began to spread slowly across all of our faces. We'd found the most awesome thing any of us could have dreamed of. This was truly, genuinely amazing!

"Er, guys," Harry began, his face turning pink.

"What's up, Harry?" asked Emma.

"Um, it's just…" continued Harry, "I mean, can we not do it now? Please? I want to, of course I do, but I'm already feeling scared and, um, a little sick, actually."

"It's okay, Harry," I said. "I totally understand. It was weird and frightening. Maybe we should wait a little until we all feel steady again. It's got to be all of us or none of us."

Everyone nodded.

"Thanks, guys," mumbled Harry.

"Let's think about it overnight," said Keith. "We can meet up here tomorrow to plan our first adventure!"

"Tomorrow," we agreed.

Chapter 3:
We Are the Tree House Club

The next day, I met Emma after school to walk to the treehouse. Harry caught up with us, puffing and red-faced, his glasses slightly steamed up.

"I'm so buzzed about this, guys!" he said. "When I woke up this morning, I thought I'd dreamt the whole thing! But it's real, isn't it?"

"It is," I smiled. "I can't wait to see it again!"

When we reached the clearing, Aaron and Keith were already there. They did not look happy.

"I told you it was too good to be true," Aaron muttered, blowing at his fringe. "It's like we all imagined it. Is that even possible?"

Keith looked troubled. "I just don't know, dude. I just don't know."

"What are you talking about?" asked Harry. He looked around and saw what Keith and Aaron had noticed. Or rather, he didn't see it.

The treehouse was gone! "How can it not be there?" He

sounded as if he were about to cry.

"It's the right place," Emma pointed out. "The right clearing, the right tree, but," she walked around the tree, "no ladder."

I felt sick to my stomach with disappointment; we all did. Then Emma said, "Let's think about what happened yesterday when Harry found the ladder."

"Yes! Harry, can you do a walk-through of exactly what you did?" suggested Keith.

"Uh, okay," replied Harry. "So, I ran into the clearing like this." He jogged to the path and started retracing his steps. "Then I ran 'round for a bit, then I hid behind the tree." We all watched him repeat his actions. Nothing.

"Anything else?" demanded Emma. "Did you think or say anything?"

"Ummm, oh yeah!" exclaimed Harry. "I shut my eyes and said, 'Please, please, don't let them find...'"

As Harry said the word "find," the ladder appeared! One second it wasn't there, and the next...it was!

"Wow!" Harry said, laughing nervously, "I did magic!"

"Yes!" said Emma excitedly. "You really did! Now let's think this through. Harry, the ladder appeared when you said 'find.' It's something to do with finding and maybe to do with shutting your eyes."

"For now," said Aaron, "let's just get up there!"

We all scrambled up the ladder and piled into the tree-house. It was exactly how I remembered it.

"Oh yeah, I almost forgot," said Keith. "We brought some

stuff to make it more comfortable."

"And then forgot about it," added Aaron. "I'll get it."

"I'll help," said Keith.

They climbed down, and I watched them through a window as they crossed the clearing and picked up the four black trash bags they'd dropped when they had first discovered the treehouse was missing. They walked back to the tree, carrying the bags over their shoulders with impressive ease. As they reached the foot of the tree, they stopped and looked at each other, bewildered.

Keith said, "No. Way."

"We were only gone a minute!" groaned Aaron.

"What's up, guys?" I shouted.

"We can't see the ladder!" replied Keith.

"Or you!" added Aaron.

"Come on," said Emma and led the way onto the platform surrounding the treehouse.

"Can you see us now?" she called.

"What the...," said Aaron and Keith together.

"You're like... we can see your heads, but no treehouse or ladder!" shouted Keith. "It's like it's hiding!"

As Keith said "hiding," Aaron said, "Whoa! There it is!"

Once Keith and Aaron were back in the treehouse, we put our heads together.

"It looks like we need a password," said Emma. "Something like 'hiding' or 'find.'"

"How about 'finders keepers'?" I suggested.

"Or 'hiders weepers'?!" laughed Harry.

"Not funny, dude, considering what we saw yesterday," said Keith, frowning.

Harry blushed, "No, I'm sorry, I didn't think." We all thought for a moment, but it was Harry who spoke up first. "I know, how about, 'You'll never find me in time'?"

"In time for what?" asked Aaron.

"Wait, that's perfect!" Emma jumped in. "Get it? Because the treehouse lets us time travel, we get to learn things that happened in time. Besides, anyone who heard us say 'find me in time' probably wouldn't be suspicious. Good thinking, Harry." She grinned.

Harry blushed, but we could all tell he was excited. We agreed that "find me in time" would be the perfect password.

"Something else we should think about," said Emma, "is how completely new all of this is. Harry was right to be cautious." She smiled kindly at Harry, who blushed again. "I think we need some time to get our heads around it," continued Emma. "I vote we wait until the weekend to go on an actual adventure."

We all voted to wait until Saturday to try out any of our time-traveling ideas.

Harry said, cheering up some, "And, of course, we need to get some supplies! So, what's in the trash bags?"

"These are beanbags!" Aaron said, pointing to three of the bags, "and I am the carrier of the beans! Well, the poly beads that go inside. I'll bring more tomorrow. My dad can get them from his work."

"And these," announced Keith, "are for us too."

He reached into the fourth bag and took out five T-shirts, all in different colors. Each T-shirt had the letters THC in the shape of a treehouse printed on the front.

"Mom has these transfer things that go through our printer. I stayed up last night and made one for each of us!" he explained.

"Cool!" Aaron said, reaching for the gray T-shirt. "What's THC?"

"It's us!" replied Keith.

"Us?" I asked.

"The Tree House Club!" Keith declared. "Welcome to the first meeting!"

Every day for the rest of the week, we met at the treehouse. We tore home from school and changed into our club T-shirts, then raced to the woods. Our password, "find me in time," seemed to work, and we each took a turn at using it to make the ladder appear.

We all brought stuff to make the treehouse feel more like our own clubhouse. Aaron brought more beanbags, and we all brought rugs to make them more comfortable. Harry found a couple of crates to use as tables, and Emma borrowed some cooler boxes from her parents' camping kit. Keith turned up with a globe, and I brought my microscope from home and some of my grandma's amazing cookies, with a promise of more to come! Between us, we soon filled the coolers with drinks and snacks. Before we knew it, it was Saturday.

This was it! The day we'd been waiting for. The day we'd agreed to go on another time-traveling adventure.

We sat in a circle in the center of the treehouse. We'd talked over our ideas about where we could go next, and we were excited about finally deciding on one of them.

"I think we need a plan first," urged Keith.

"I agree," said Emma. "We don't know exactly how this works or what might happen."

"Or how we get back," I added.

We all nodded—that is, all except Aaron.

"I want to go to the Alamo in March 1836 when the Texans tried to hold off the Mexicans!" he blurted.

No sooner had the words left his mouth than the floor started vibrating with a deep rumbling sound. Lights started flashing in the windows.

They flashed faster and faster as the whole treehouse shook. Then everything went dark. When the walls reappeared, they weren't wooden anymore but gray stone. The air was full of bitter-smelling smoke that reminded me a little of fireworks.

Everywhere, men in filthy blue jackets and white trousers were running and shouting. There was a constant sound of bullets striking stone and deeper explosions that shook the walls and floor. At a window carved roughly out of the stone wall, a man in a furry hat was peering down his rifle, but he didn't shoot.

"More Mexicans comin'!" he shouted. "More men over here! To me! To me!"

I looked around at my friends. They were frozen to the spot and grim-faced. Harry looked as if he might puke. I wondered if we were invisible like we had been the last time. I soon found out.

A man with enormous side whiskers seemed to be in charge. He'd taken off his uniform jacket and wore just a white shirt, but he was shouting orders from the center of the room and soldiers were leaping to follow his commands.

"CANNON!" he roared. "You men," he bawled at us, "get

away from that wall. It's gonna come down!"

"Men?" shouted Keith over the uproar. "You still see me in my T-shirt, right?"

We all nodded.

"But *he*," Keith indicated with his head, "sees soldiers. To him, we're just like them." Before we could consider this, the man yelled again. "Away from the wall! Get back! Get back! Get back!"

43

Chapter 4:
A Dangerous Game

At exactly the moment the man stopped shouting, there was a massive, deafening BOOM! I felt it before I heard it. The wall nearest to us buckled in what seemed like slow motion and just...disintegrated. Huge fragments of stone spun through the dusty air toward us. We all screamed, dove for the floor, and —WHOOSH! We were back in the treehouse again.

Shaking and pale, we patted our arms, legs and heads, checking for damage. It felt like a miracle that we weren't injured.

"Well, that was—" began Keith.

"Absolutely terrifying!" Emma interrupted. "War is horrible! I've never been so scared!"

"Nor me!" I agreed.

"I feel sick," stated Harry. "Also a bit hungry. Weird."

Aaron still hadn't said anything. His usually pale face was entirely drained of color.

"Guys, I'm—" he started, then his voice broke, and he started trembling uncontrollably. "I'm...so...sorry!" he managed to get out between big gulps of air.

Emma snapped, "So you should be!" Then, more kindly, "It was a mistake, wasn't it? I mean, you didn't mean it to happen straight away like that, did you?"

Aaron shook his head. "I would never–never–put you all in danger."

"That's why we need a plan in the future," said Keith.

"And also to be very careful what we wish for—in here, at least," I added.

Like Harry, we were all weirdly hungry, so we had a snack. Then we discussed what had happened.

"It's strange. Before, when we saw the family hiding up here, it was in the past, but we were like ghosts. They couldn't see us or hear us," I observed, tugging at my puffy hair.

"But this time, we were actually there"— nodded Emma— "at the Alamo." She shivered.

"That soldier, the one who was in charge, he saw us!" marveled Harry.

"But he didn't see us, did he?" said Keith. "That's what I've been thinking about. He saw soldiers. To him, we were just more of his men."

We all murmured our agreement.

"D'you know who I think that was?" said Aaron. "I think it was James Bowie. I mean, he was in charge at the Alamo, wasn't he?"

"Or maybe it was Colonel Travis," suggested Emma.

"And the other guy, in the fur hat—I think that was Davy Crockett!" piped up Harry.

"It should have been exciting," said Aaron, still slightly ashamed.

"I love your sense of adventure, Aaron," Emma said, "but let's plan a little so we know what we're dropping into next time. You weren't clear enough with the date, so we ended up just before the Alamo was overrun. No one survived!"

"I did?" Aaron said. "Oh, shoot! I looked it up, and it just said March 1836. Maybe I should've read a little more. But, Davy Crockett! Whoa!"

We all had to smile at that. It had been amazing to see Davy Crockett!

"Okay, let's make a proper plan!" said Keith.

"Let's think about what we already know," suggested Emma. She counted off points on her fingers as she spoke. "One, we end up exactly where we ask to go if we say an exact place. Two, we end up when we ask to be, so we need to be super clear about dates in the future," she said, smiling at Aaron. "Three, in the past, people can sometimes see us and hear us. Four, to them, we look like them, but we still look like us to each other. I wonder if that's always going to happen."

"Five—and this is important, guys," I said, "the treehouse brings us back if we're in real danger. I think. I hope!" There was general agreement about this.

"Something I thought about," said Aaron, "is the lights flashing on and off. It's like the sun coming up and going down, but super-speeded up. Do you think they're days? They lasted longer when we visited the Alamo than the last time."

"Yeah, about that," added Harry, "I was wearing my

watch at the Alamo. We left at 11a.m. When we got back, it was...11a.m.!"

"So time doesn't pass here when we're in the past," mused Emma. "Interesting. I wonder if it always works that way."

"There are still some things we don't know for sure," said Keith, "like if the people in the past can always see us and if we always look like them. But I guess the only way to find out is to try it again. Safely, this time," he added with a nod and a grin to Aaron.

"Okay, so where should we go?" Emma asked us.

Harry picked up his backpack and pulled out a piece of paper. He carefully unfolded it, smoothing out the creases so we could all see it. I recognized a rendering of Christopher Columbus on his ship, which Harry had cut out of a magazine.

"I just thought," he started. "I just thought, wouldn't it be awesome to go back to the very beginning of America? To when Columbus landed?"

We looked at the picture, then at each other, then back at the picture. The image of the man who many people thought had discovered America stared back at us.

"I don't know if we'll be able to find the exact time it happened," mused Keith, "but maybe we could ask the treehouse to take us back to just before Columbus landed."

"It would be cool to see Columbus actually coming to shore!" I agreed.

"And we'd get to see what the island was like before Europeans got there," added Emma.

Then we all started talking at once.

"We need to find out more about the people who were there already."

"It was somewhere in the Caribbean, wasn't it?"

"Yes! I can't remember the name of the island, though. Or

the Native American tribe."

"We need to do some more research!"

"Let's decide who looks up what!"

"And tomorrow, we can try it out!" Keith looked around, grinning hugely.

"It's a plan!" I said.

"It's a master plan!" said Harry.

"It's a masterful master plan!" Emma added.

"Well, it's alright, I guess," Aaron said with a smirk, and everyone laughed.

***

The next day, Sunday, we all sat in a circle in the center of the treehouse.

"Okay, guys, what've we found out?" asked Keith.

"I found out about Columbus!" said Harry excitedly. "He was an amazing explorer! He wanted to discover new lands—just like us!"

"It sure was an incredible voyage," added Keith, "because the only map he could've seen was half made-up! It had all kinds of monsters and legends on it, and people thought the ocean just went on for months. Which means he must have been pretty brave," he added, nodding at Harry.

"All that way in three little ships," agreed Aaron. "Some of them were barely bigger than the treehouse—the inside of it anyway! They were at sea for thirty-six days. They must have been getting desperate to see land!"

"He called the island he found 'San Salvador,'" said Emma, "but the people who already lived there called it Guanahani. They called themselves the Taino Lukku-Cairi, which means 'people of the islands.'"

"But why did he travel so far?" I asked.

"I read that Columbus was only looking for gold and new land to farm. So did he just want to get rich?"

Emma nodded. "I read that he wanted to make all the people he met work for him as servants. Or even slaves," she said, shaking her head.

"That doesn't sound very heroic," said Keith.

"Hmmm, maybe some of our ideas about him are a little off…," added Aaron.

"But he wanted to make maps too!" objected Harry. "And to explore the world so other people could follow him. He's still a hero to me!"

"I guess the only way to find out for sure is to see it for ourselves," said Emma.

We all agreed. We felt as ready as we'd ever be for our next adventure. I noticed Aaron fidgeting and realized that everyone was probably as nervous as I was.

"Remember, we need to try not to be seen, okay?" Keith ordered. "We're not really sure what we look like to these people. It could be weird!"

We nodded, and Keith began.

"Treehouse, we want to go back to 1492, just before Columbus's ships arrived in Guanahani."

The rumbling started as the floor began to shake, and lights flashed faster and faster. Then everything went dark…

This time, the shaking and flashing lights carried on much longer than before. Very slowly, as if coming into focus, the treehouse disappeared, and the space around us turned into a mixture of soft blues and greens. The colors grew clearer and sharper, and soon we could make out trees, the sea, and a cloudy sky very early in the morning. We were on an island!

"Ugh. Can someone help me?" Harry groaned.

Somehow, he'd ended up headfirst in a prickly bush. We could only see his legs waving about frantically.

Aaron and Keith, giggling, pulled him out and onto his feet. Keith brushed him down. Covered in leaves and twigs, Harry looked a lot like a bush himself!

"So, is it time to explore now?" Emma asked.

We all nodded and looked around.

We'd arrived in a thick forest at the edge of a beach. We walked out from under the trees to get a better sense of where we were. The beach was a long wide strip of white sand. The sea beyond was covered with white-topped waves and was the bluest blue I'd ever seen.

We were all wearing our THC T-shirts and shorts. The shorts had been Emma's idea; she'd realized it would be seriously hot on the island. Well, we weren't going to lose each other thanks to our brightly colored T-shirts, but it would be difficult to blend in! Except for Aaron, whose T-shirt was gray, we looked like we'd landed from another planet. In a way, I guess we had.

"Maybe you should explore on your own, Keith," said Emma. "Just have a quick look around. It'll be easier for you to stay hidden by yourself."

"Okay," he agreed, "I'll only be a few minutes. I'll meet you back here."

We watched as Keith walked away along the sand, staying close to the trees. It was a smart move—he could hide quickly if someone appeared. The beach looked pretty long from where we were. We could make out some big rocks at the opposite end, and beyond them, we could see more forest. Keith climbed over the rocks, and that was the last we saw of him until he came racing back about twenty minutes later, waving and calling to us.

"Guys, guys, it's okay! It's fine! It's really—" He reached us and stopped, panting with his hands on his knees.

"Why don't you take a few breaths, then tell us what happened?" suggested Emma.

A minute later, we all sat on the sand while Keith told us what he'd seen. When he'd climbed over the rocks, he'd come out on the other side into a clearing full of people! And they could all see him!

"I froze! I knew that running back the way I came could be a big mistake because I'd lead them straight to you guys. But standing there in my bright red T-shirt and khaki shorts didn't seem like such a great idea either! I mean, they didn't look like anyone I'd ever seen, and I guessed I looked just as strange to them."

"What did they look like?" asked Emma.

"They weren't wearing many clothes," said Keith, blushing slightly, "and they had feathers in their hair and paint on their faces and bodies." He paused thoughtfully, then shook his head. "Anyhow," he continued, "it was then that something really, really strange happened… Nothing!"

"Huh? What do you mean?" I asked.

"I mean, nothing! They all looked up when I appeared, then carried on as if there was nothing out of the ordinary. Not one of them looked surprised by the way I was dressed or my hair or anything! Then this one guy came up to me, did a little bow and said, 'Hello, my friend.'"

Keith's amazement that he'd understood the man was clear. Keith described how he'd bowed back and said hello—in English—and the man had smiled and walked away. Our friend then walked on, and women and children had come to meet him, clasping his hands, bowing their heads and smiling. They'd brought him gifts of flowers and fruit and had guided him through a village of circular wooden huts.

"They offered me a bowl of water, which I really needed by then," he continued. "But when I looked down into the bowl, I saw my reflection, and that was just the weirdest thing ever. It wasn't my face, guys! I looked just like them! I mean, I still looked like me, but my skin was lighter brown and I had feathers in my hair and face paint, like them! And my hair"— he touched his buzz-cut self-consciously—"wasn't the same, either, it was longer and straighter, like theirs!"

Keith's astonished gasp had made the tribespeople scurry around to find a new drinking bowl, thinking that he was reacting to the one he'd been given. That had given him a few moments to try to work out exactly what was going on.

Somehow, he realized, he'd found himself in the middle of a tribe of Taino people from hundreds of years ago. They seemed to see him as an important visitor. He looked like them, he could understand their language, and they could understand him too.

"So I said to them, 'I would like to bring my people here!'" Keith said. "It's what I thought a Taino leader would say," he

added sheepishly.

"So we're your people now, are we, oh great chieftain?" sniped Aaron.

We laughed.

"Do you think it'll be the same for us? Will we look like them?" I asked.

"Even us very pale ones?" joked Harry, tugging on his

light reddish hair.

"Well, they said we'd be welcome, so I guess we might as well try," replied Keith.

"Let's go meet them!"

Chapter 6:
Part of the Tribe

Aaron, impatient as usual, had wandered out onto the beach.

"Come on!" he shouted back to us. "Let's go already!"

The shore stretched out along the long, sandy beach, and the white sand we walked on shimmered in the morning sun. On one side, the ocean spread far to the horizon, while on the other, the forest threw its cool green shade. When we scrambled to the top of the rocks at the other end of the beach, we saw the clearing that Keith had described.

"Wow!" breathed Harry. "This is like a movie or something!"

"The Land Before Time!" laughed Emma.

We could see a few people moving about in the clearing below us.

"Well, here goes!" said Aaron, starting to climb down the other side of the rocks.

"I should go first," Keith said. "I think they see me as the one in charge."

Aaron scowled slightly but let Keith lead the way.

The tribespeople turned to us with smiles of welcome and

soft greetings as we arrived. They followed us as we wandered through the clearing, heading toward the Taino huts that were tucked under the trees.

"Still nervous?" Keith asked me.

"A little," I said.

We were very quiet as we approached the Taino village. I think we'd all heard stories about the original tribes of the Americas and how warlike and bloodthirsty they were supposed to have been. Only Emma seemed calm.

"The treehouse will take us back home if it gets too dangerous, right?" I murmured.

"It's fine," insisted Keith. "They were really friendly to me before. Even if we didn't look and sound like them, I think we'd be safe. Honest."

We followed Keith through the entrance to the village, which was marked by two enormous posts covered with carvings of animals and people.

We stopped and looked around us. The village wasn't large, just a dozen round huts made of branches, with sloping triangular roofs. The huts surrounded a big circle of smooth rounded stones, each large enough to sit on. A fire pit was built in the center of the circle, but it wasn't lit.

"That must be their meeting place," said Emma.

There weren't any men around the camp. A few women and children were working in the doorways of huts, preparing food and working on what looked like cotton nets and cloth. Some kids around our age were collecting berries and fruit on big leaves at the edge of the forest.

When they saw us, everyone stopped what they were do-ing and walked over to us. It was the moment of truth! Would they accept us the same way that they'd accepted Keith?

"Oohhh," moaned Harry softly.

"Shh, it's okay," I said. "Look, they're all smiling."

And they were. All the tribespeople seemed overjoyed to see us as if we were good friends they hadn't seen for a long time. A couple of women led us into a hut with no furniture

aside from some hammocks. They told us we could rest there after our long journey. We heard happy shouts and laughter from outside and returned to the fire pit.

Some men had returned to the village. We watched as a man in a wonderful headdress strode toward the fire pit. The headdress was made of the most beautiful colored feathers I'd ever seen. It framed the man's head like the rays of the sun. He was followed by around twenty men dressed, as he was, in cloths around their hips, and most were carrying bundles of leaves tied up with cords. They also carried long, fierce-looking wooden spears!

I saw Harry and Aaron turn tense and pale. Even Keith looked uncertain of what was going to happen next. The man in the headdress walked straight over to Keith, grasped him by the shoulders and shook him.

"Good—you came back! I am Tiburon, and these are my people."

The chief held out his arms wide to include all the tribespeople. Then he crossed the circle of stones and sat down on a seat hollowed out of a huge log.

"Please, stay and eat with us!" He gestured to the men who had appeared with him, and they unwrapped the bundles of leaves to reveal a variety of fish. A couple of women set about lighting the fire while the men sat on stones and cleaned the fish.

"That was what the spears were for!" whispered Emma. "I read about spear-fishing before we came, but I didn't have a chance to tell you guys."

Keith thanked Tiburon, then shuffled his feet and cleared his throat a couple of times before saying, "I am Keith. This is Emma, Aaron, Harry, and Ashley. We are a small group who travel from place to place, learning about our land."

"Nice moves!" murmured Aaron. "That's pretty much what we are."

"Your names are... unusual," replied Tiburon, "but you're all welcome!"

We were all invited to sit on stones in the circle. Keith was shown to a wooden seat, similar to Tiburon's, shaped from a single block of wood. One end was beautifully carved in the shape of an animal's head.

"That chair is amazing!" Emma said softly. "It must have taken so much skill to make it so lifelike."

"Thank you!" replied a woman standing close by. "That's our duho. It's reserved for our special guests."

Another woman walked over with bowls of water for us. "I'm Aramana. Welcome to our village. Please, have some water. You must be thirsty."

Emma sipped and smiled, "Thank you so much." She turned to me, saying quietly, "These people are amazing. Everything here feels kind of special. It's hard to explain...," she trailed off.

"You're right," I answered, "I feel it too. Look at all those beautiful things made out of shells and bones hanging everywhere. It's like everything has its own magic."

"Hey!" came a sudden shout from the beach. "Everyone, come here! Come now!"

The men sitting around the circle rose swiftly.

We all did the same.

What was happening? Could this be the moment we'd come here to see?

We all rushed onto the sand with the rest of the tribe. There, on the other side of the reef, bobbed three ships.

"D'you think that's him?" breathed Harry.

It must be," whispered Keith, who'd found out all about Columbus's voyage. "He had three ships—the Niña, the Pinta, and the Santa Maria. That has to be them!"

Keith went to stand beside Tiburon.

"More visitors!" said the chief. "It's our lucky day!"

"You should be careful, my friend," said Keith.

"Nonsense!" Tiburon declared. "We'll welcome them! They probably want to trade with us. Quickly, bring out our goods!"

Soon there was a carpet of objects on the shore around the chief's feet. There were flowers and ferns from the forest, meat and fish, dozens of painted amulets made of stone and shell, newly-carved wooden spears, rolls of cloth, cotton string, and even a few dozen parrots tied to perches.

"These are beautiful!" I exclaimed, kneeling to sift through the amulets. "How have you made them? So clever!"

"Would you like one?" asked a Taino woman, kneeling beside me. "My name is Ana. I made these—I'd like you to have one."

"Really? That would be wonderful!"

Ana lifted a necklace of carved shells and pebbles from the pile, then hung it around my neck. I couldn't speak; I stroked the gift gently.

"Thank you," I said. "Thank you so much."

By this time, the ships in the distance had stowed their sails and dropped anchor half a mile from shore. They looked so small; I was impressed that they'd traveled so far. I could just make out the carved bow of one of them and knew that it must be Columbus's ship.

A rowboat left the largest ship. At first, it looked like a bird bobbing on the waves, but it soon grew larger as it got closer.

"Do you think that's him?!" exclaimed Harry, squinting to see more clearly against the glare of the sea. Five men stood in the boat, which was being rowed by ten more men.

"Er, guys," remarked Aaron, "they're all carrying swords."

"Swords!" Harry squealed faintly.

"They're carrying weapons," Keith said, turning to Tiburon.

The chief laughed, "Of course! We carry weapons too when we visit other islands to trade. You never know what you might find."

I saw Harry edge toward the back of the crowd of tribespeople. He shot me an apologetic look.

As they got closer, it was clear that the men rowing the boat hadn't had healthy food in a while. They were thin and had dark shadows under their eyes. They may have been tanned from being at sea, but they didn't look healthy. They looked like hungry dogs.

The men who were standing wore capes and hats with feathers. Buttons shone on their tunics.

The men rowing the boats were not dressed smartly, and some of their clothes were more like rags.

One man glared proudly at the island as he stood in the prow of the boat, hands on his hips.

"Yep, that must be him," said Aaron, so quietly that only I could hear him.

When the boat landed on the sand, the men jumped out to pull it further up the beach. One rower carried the well-dressed man on his back up to the dry sand, careful not to let the man's shoes get wet. He lowered him gently in front of the tribespeople.

The man who had been carried ashore signaled to one of his men, who ran up and pushed a flagpole into the sand. As the red and yellow flag flapped on its pole, the man raised his sword and all the strangers cheered.

"I am Christopher Columbus, and I claim this island for

Queen Isabella!" shouted the man. "It is ours by right, and these people agree that it is ours!"

The large flag waved in the breeze, and Columbus put away his sword and turned to one of his officers.

"These people look strong and healthy. They will make useful laborers. The land looks fertile and good for farming as well! Excellent!"

I saw Keith tense up when he heard Columbus's remarks, but he didn't say anything.

Even though Columbus was speaking in Spanish, our tree-house powers meant that we could understand every word he said. The Taino tribespeople couldn't, of course, so they took his smiles as a good sign and beamed back at him in welcome.

"Welcome to our island!" said Tiburon with a broad smile.

The Spanish sailors were growing louder and overexcited. They saw the fresh food laid out along the shore and were clearly desperate to fill their empty bellies.

Columbus quieted them with a raised hand.

"Peace, men! We'll find out exactly what these Indians have to offer us."

He approached Chief Tiburon with a swagger and stopped in front of him, his hand on his sword.

Emma gasped, "Oh no!" very quietly. I held my breath.

Chapter 8:
I Am Columbus!

Columbus stood in front of Tiburon, who continued to smile in a friendly way as he pointed toward the pile of goods beside him.

"We have plenty of goods to trade with you," Tiburon said, "but what have you got to trade with us?"

"This is all trash!" snorted Columbus, glaring at the Taino goods. "I'm sure you have gold here somewhere," he mused.

Tiburon only looked at him questioningly.

"Metal, like this," he said, drawing his sword.

Tiburon's eyes widened as the sun sparkled on the blade of Columbus's sword.

"That's beautiful!" he exclaimed. "Such wonderful carving! This is worth a hundred parrots!"

He reached out and grasped the end of the blade. Scowling, Columbus quickly pulled the sword out of Tiburon's hand, and the sharp edge of the sword cut into Tiburon's skin. His hand started bleeding heavily, the drops spattering the sand at his feet.

Columbus and the Spanish sailors laughed.

Tiburon's face crinkled in embarrassment and pain.

"How stupid of me!" he declared. "There must be another way to hold it."

He reached out again, this time toward the handle of Columbus's sword. Columbus put his hand out to stop Tiburon and put the sword away, saying, "These ignorant natives will be easy to fool! We'll return tomorrow with some trinkets to trade with them! For now, men, fill your bellies!"

Columbus beckoned, and the Spanish sailors moved quickly toward the tribe. Greedily, they gathered up the food, eating it as they went and discussing the great feast they'd have later. They threw the beautifully crafted Taino amulets aside with disgust, calling them "junk!" or "useless!" Soon they were rowing their boat back toward the ships on the horizon.

The Taino were confused by the behavior of the Spanish sailors, but they allowed them to take the food and leave.

We followed the tribespeople back to their village, where we ate fruit and freshly cooked fish. Tiburon asked us if we'd seen the strangers before, and we all felt terrible about having to pretend they were strangers to us as well. Later that night, in our hammocks, we discussed what we could do to help the Taino.

"The way I see it, we can't do anything," argued Aaron. "I mean, this happened, right?"

"Let's just wait and see what Columbus does," said Harry stubbornly. "I can't believe he really means them any harm."

"He hasn't got any respect for them, though, has he?" I asked.

"No. He just doesn't see what we see," said Emma sadly.

***

The next day, the rowboat carrying Columbus and his men reappeared at the shore. We were there with Tiburon and the tribespeople to greet them.

"Welcome back," said Tiburon, more cautious this time. "What have you brought to trade with us?"

Columbus gestured to some of the men. They set a large chest in front of Tiburon. When they opened it, we saw that it was filled with everyday stuff: some leather hats and belts, strings of glass beads and brass bells.

The tribespeople gathered around the chest, pulling out objects with murmurs of delight.

"Wow," said Aaron softly, "they're really behaving as if it's treasure. It's just junk."

"But it's new to them," replied Emma, "so I guess it is like treasure."

Some of the Taino men and women were trying on the hats, all but ignoring the Spanish sailors who stood around, laughing quietly and making rude comments. It was tough to watch them mocking our new friends.

Finally, one of the Spanish sailors started trying to communicate with Tiburon while Columbus looked on. He held out a gold coin in his hand, then raised his eyebrows questioningly and opened his arms to indicate the island.

"Gold," he said. "Where is gold?"

"They want more of this shining stuff, I think. But there's none here," replied Tiburon, shaking his head at the Spanish sailor. "Some tribes on other islands have this," he said slowly, pointing toward the sea, "but we don't use it."

"What's that?" interrupted Columbus sharply.

"I think, sir, that he's saying there's gold somewhere else," answered the sailor.

"Then they can show us where it is!" said Columbus trium-phantly. "Get the boat ready and get them to agree to guide us—in exchange for more treasure, of course," he smirked, gesturing at the cheap trinkets he had brought for trading.

The Spanish sailor managed to communicate this to Tiburon, who agreed.

"Tomorrow," he said, "we'll send two canoes with you." He gestured at the long canoes further down the beach, and a dozen of the Taino men nodded in agreement.

"Tell him we want some men to come on board our ship," said Columbus to the sailor. "I want to take some specimens back with us. We'll see if these heathens can be turned into proper Christian men on the voyage."

"What?!" spluttered Keith.

"He's kidnapping them!" I said.

"But he can't!" said Harry. "I mean, he's only exploring…" He looked at us pleadingly. "Isn't he?"

"I guess not, Harry," replied Emma, shaking her head.

"Well, I'm not standing for it," said Aaron, and before we could stop him, he was marching toward Columbus!

"Now look here—" he started to say.

Columbus's men turned and stared in amazement.

"That one speaks Spanish! But how?" said the sailor who'd been talking to Tiburon.

"Never mind that—grab him!" shouted Columbus. "He can translate for us!"

Three Spanish sailors rushed toward Aaron with their

arms out. Just as they were about to reach him, the ground began to shake...

Chapter 9:
A Sad Return

It all happened so suddenly—one moment we were on the beach, surrounded by Columbus's men and the Taino, and the next, they'd all disappeared. Lights flashed, faster and faster, and I felt a huge jolt as the ground seemed to fly up to meet me. Before I had time to make any sense of it all, I found myself on a beanbag back in the treehouse.

"Is everyone here? Did everyone get out?" came Keith's voice through the ringing in my ears.

"Y-yes," I replied shakily, and I was relieved to hear everyone else say the same.

"Wow! That was even bumpier than the Alamo!" Emma said.

"It was super scary...," said Harry.

"It was too close!" I declared.

"What's the time?" asked Emma.

"Just past 1 p.m.," Harry replied. "Exactly when we left."

"Phew!" I breathed. "At least we were right about that!"

Keith and Aaron were silent. Keith was staring at Aaron,

but Aaron wasn't looking in his direction. Nobody spoke for a long while. We all waited for one of them to break the long silence.

Aaron went first, muttering as he stared at the floor. "It was too horrible; I couldn't help it!"

"It was awful!" Keith agreed. "But we had a good idea before we went, that Columbus's arrival wouldn't be good news for the Taino."

"But Columbus and his men...they acted like they owned the world!" argued Aaron.

"They wanted to kidnap the Taino," I said quietly.

"I r-really thought," gulped Harry, "that Columbus was some kind of hero, exploring the world and discovering new places."

"But really, he just wanted to find treasure and land—or people—to use!" spat Keith.

Emma said, "We've got to remember, Columbus came from a different time—a different world. The Spanish explorers didn't even see the Taino as properly human because they were so different from them."

"I feel like we should go back," said Keith, "I want to see what happened to Tiburon and his tribe. Even if it's...not good."

"Right now, all I want is to go home and see my mom and dad," said Harry.

We all murmured our agreement. Suddenly, home seemed like the best place in the world. I wanted so badly to hug my mom and snuggle up to watch a cheesy film with my dad.

"Let's meet up tomorrow after school," Keith suggested. "We can work out a plan then."

As I walked back toward home with Emma, I realized that I was still wearing the necklace that Ana had given me. The treehouse had brought it back through time! I touched it, hoping our Taino friends would somehow be saved.

***

We spent the next week meeting up at the treehouse after school, working out what to do next. Sure, we'd started out wanting to meet Columbus, but we'd discovered something even better. We all agreed to find out as much as we could about the Taino people before we made a decision.

"I found out that Columbus returned to the island three more times," Keith said.

"And even the Spanish were impressed by the Taino people eventually," Emma told us.

"Guys, I found out something awesome," I said, feeling a little shy, "my mom saw me looking up information about the Taino, and she said, 'Ah, the ancestors!'"

"What did she mean, Ash?" asked Harry.

"She said that Puerto Ricans regard the Taino as our ancestors; that we believe we're descended from the original tribes of those islands. Isn't that amazing?" I said, feeling suddenly overwhelmed by my feelings.

"Now that I think about it," said Emma, giving me a quick hug, "you did look a lot like Ana and the other women. Or they looked like you. Or something.”

"We should go back and see what happened to them,” Aaron said.

Harry nodded grimly. “Yeah, we should find out. I think it may make us sad, though.”

"Should we go back to the same time? Maybe a day or two later?” Emma asked.

"I think to find out what really happened, we need to go back to 1494, two years later,” Keith said. “Columbus returned in November 1493 and brought twelve hundred Europeans with him to live on Guanahani and the other islands. They called themselves colonists.”

 "Let's do it,” Aaron said. “And I promise not to do stupid stuff if I get angry.”

Keith nodded and smiled. We stood in a circle, and he said, “Treehouse, we want to go to Guanahani in April 1494.”

The floor began to shake…

We landed in a huge, bare, dusty yard, surrounded by tall wooden posts. The posts made a massive wall around the space, and square wooden huts were huddled at the foot of it.

"Are we in the right place?” I asked.

"I have no idea,” replied Keith. “Why would the treehouse have brought us somewhere different?”

"Look, there's a gap in the wall over there,” pointed Emma. “Let's go get our bearings.”

We walked in the direction she'd pointed and soon ran into a group of people—but they weren't tribespeople. They looked a lot like the sailors who'd been with Columbus.

"Let's just pray the treehouse magic works and we look like them," muttered Aaron.

And it did! The colonists didn't blink as we walked past them and out through the gap in the wall.

I wasn't the only one to gasp with horror and shock as we realized where we were.

"This is the same place!" exclaimed Keith.

"Although it's hard to believe," added Harry.

We were at the end of the beach, in exactly the same spot where we'd arrived before. But where the forest had been last time there were only tree stumps and sandy dirt. The trees had been cut down and used to make the huge wooden wall surrounding the colonists' settlement.

Keith nodded in the direction of the rocks at the far end of the beach, and we all trooped toward them.

"Do you think the village will still be there?" I asked.

"I'm not hopeful," replied Emma through clenched teeth. She was right not to hope. The huts were gone. The circle of stones was broken up. There was no sign that anyone at all lived there.

We looked back at the devastated land and knew that the Taino's way of life had been destroyed. But where had the Taino people gone?

A small cry made us turn in the direction of the few trees behind the village.

"My friends! You survived!" Ana emerged from the trees, smiling.

"Ana!" we rushed toward her.

"Come with me," whispered Ana. "It's not safe here anymore."

My relief at seeing Ana was doubled by the fact that she still saw us as tribespeople like herself; the treehouse magic was holding up. Ana's appearance meant that the rest of the tribe could have survived too. She silently led us deeper into the forest.

After a long walk, we came to a clearing where we saw a

small ring of stones around a fire. Beyond it, a curved line of huts had been built. Less than half of the tribespeople we'd met last time came to greet us, most of them women and children. Chief Tiburon was nowhere to be seen.

"Where's the chief?" Keith asked.

Ana bowed her head and her tears fell to the ground. "He was taken away on a boat. We haven't seen him since.

"Can you tell us what happened to the village?" asked Emma gently.

"The visitors came back, and some of them stayed here. They started attacking us, trying to make us show them where the gold was. For a while, our men fought back," continued Ana. "Then a few months ago, the visitors returned, bringing even more people."

We were stunned. We didn't know what to say about the terrible fate of the tribe.

"Lots of us were killed then," continued Ana, "but some escaped. We came here, deeper into the forest, to hide. If they find us, they'll kill us or make us work for them."

Tears were flowing down Ana's face. I wrapped my arms around her, wishing I could do something more to comfort her. I felt a strong connection to her—maybe as a distant ancestor, but also as a friend.

A rustling in the forest behind us made the tribespeople scatter. They ran to their huts, carrying the children, and came out carrying spears. Nothing had been decorated with shells or stones; these weapons were only used for self-defense.

Ana's eyes widened. "Run! Hide!"

"No, we'll stay and help!" Aaron said immediately.

"Please, go!" begged Ana. "Save yourselves!"

Chapter 10:
Between Worlds

A large group of men ran out of the trees. There must have been around forty of them, all wearing uniforms and holding long, old-fashioned guns and swords.

Had we brought them here? Had they followed us?

For a few moments, no one moved. Standing beside the Taino people, we turned to face the soldiers.

"What are you doing here?" one of them shouted angrily to Aaron and Harry.

"And you women too! Why are you there?" another shouted, pointing at Emma and me.

"They think we are colonists," Keith said.

"Maybe they won't attack us then," suggested Emma.

"Or they might try to kill all the tribespeople because they think they're holding us prisoner!"

"Let's walk toward them and try to stay between them and the Taino," Aaron suggested.

"It's too dangerous!" said Keith.

"Not if they think we're colonists. If it gets too dangerous, the treehouse will take us back," Aaron argued.

"Will it? Do we know that for sure?" I asked.

The soldiers looked with disgust at the tribespeople.

"It's like they don't even see them as human," said Emma.

"Idiots!" growled Aaron.

"Right, let's walk toward them!" Keith said.

"No, no, stay with us; we'll protect you!" Ana cried, seeing us move toward the soldiers.

We all carried on walking slowly. Could this possibly work?

We were soon to find out. From behind us, the Taino tribe yelled and charged forward, spears held high, to protect us.

Seconds later, the Spanish soldiers charged also, guns pointed and swords raised. We were caught right in the middle.

Keith had just enough time to hold out both his hands in a doomed attempt to stop each side before the ground began to shake…

…We were all safely back in the treehouse. The magic had worked in time to save us. Not one of us felt good about this. We knew our friends couldn't possibly have survived their battle with the Spanish soldiers.

***

It took a while for us to want to hang out at the treehouse again. One day, Keith asked us to meet him there. I turned up first with Emma.

"Oh, Keith! I love it," she said.

I couldn't speak; I just smiled and nodded through my tears. Then Harry's head appeared at the top of the ladder.

"Wow, that looks awesome!" he said, coming inside.

Aaron appeared last. "Amazing!" he exclaimed.

Around the edge of the room, five hammocks were hanging from the ceiling. They weren't exactly the same, but they were pretty close to the ones the Taino had used. Keith had found out that even the word "hammock" originally came from the Taino people.

Keith had also painted images of the animals and Gods of the Taino on one of the walls of the treehouse.

"I just thought," he said, "that, well, we couldn't save our Taino friends, but we can keep some of their ideas alive."

"Keith, it's perfect," I said, touching my favorite shell on my necklace and thinking about Ana and the rest of my ancestors.

"When I grow up," declared Emma, "I'm going to make sure everyone knows about how awesome the Taino people were." There was a gleam in her eye that made it impossible to doubt her.

"I can't believe," grumbled Harry, "that we still celebrate Columbus Day. After what he did to the Taino!"

"Ha! I found out something cool about that, actually," said Aaron. "People were discriminating against the first Italian immigrants to come to America, so they started the tradition of Columbus Day."

We all looked at him, confused.

"Don't you see?" he grinned, "Columbus was from Genoa. In *Italy.* His real name was Cristoforo Colombo. The first Italian Americans were making a link between the guy who 'discovered' America and them so people would accept them. Brilliant, really!"

***

After that, we started meeting up at the treehouse regularly again. Over the summer vacation, we spent almost every day there. It started to feel like our clubhouse, and I guess we

forgot its magical time-traveling power, just a little.

One afternoon, just after the start of the new school year, we started talking about another adventure.

"Can we please, please, not go anywhere there's going to

be fighting?" moaned Harry.

"It's so not fun when it's terrifying!" Emma agreed.

"Or heartbreaking," I added.

"You know what?" said Aaron. "I think I may have an idea. My class at school is doing a project on inventions that changed the world. I already decided that my project is going to be on the moon landings."

"Ooh," said Harry, his eyebrows shooting upwards, "you mean, go to the moon?!"

When we'd all finished laughing, Keith said, "I don't think even the treehouse is that magical, Harry!"

"But getting involved somehow in the Apollo Eleven space mission?" mused Emma. "You know, Aaron, that's a brilliant idea!"

We all agreed, and—remembering how dangerous a lack of knowledge could be—we spent the rest of the week finding out as much as we could about Apollo Eleven and the very first moon landing. Soon we would be ready for our next adventure!

Don't miss out on their next adventure!

The Tree House Club is off to see history being made – all the way to Houston in 1969, for a ringside seat at the Apollo Eleven space mission! As usual, things don't turn out exactly as they expect...

  Follow the Tree House Club as they discover that there's more to the space race than they think they know!

FIND ME IN TIME
MISSION APOLLO
L.T. CATON

About the Author

Children's book author L.T. Caton knew early in her teaching career that she wanted to be a writer. As a young student, history was her least favorite subject because she found it boring and often questioned why the historical facts in textbooks provided one perspective.

As a teacher and writer, L.T.'s goal is to educate students in a fun way about people in history who are often not mentioned in textbooks and explore the many conflicting versions of history. She hopes to achieve this goal through the book series, *Find Me in Time,* a collection of chapter books covering significant historical events or periods.

L.T. thinks a great book has relatable characters, an engaging plot, and a lesson learned that can be applied to real-life long after the book is closed. She hopes her books inspire a love of reading and, in particular, motivate children of color and young girls to learn about people in history who look like them.

Hailing from New York, when she's not writing fascinating historical fiction stories for young readers, L.T. enjoys being near the ocean—fishing, walking on the beach, sailing, and cycling. She also enjoys baking, cooking, traveling, community service, and being with family and friends. Her family, including her parents, sister, and late maternal grandmother, have supported her professional journey.

Find Me in Time's debut title is Meeting Columbus, about the famed explorer's first landing in the New World.